For Arthur

Bagheera lives in an old cottage in Cornwall.

Bagheera thinks he is a black panther but really he is a fluffy black cat.

Bagheera wants to go hunting in the jungle for wild animals.

There are two main problems with this idea.

Firstly, there are no tropical rainforests in Cornwall.

Secondly, it is tricky to hunt in the jungle when you have a ...

Bagheera wants to hunt for jungle birds.

"Perhaps", he thinks,
"I will catch a great hornbill
or maybe a drongo".

There are at least two problems with this.

Firstly, there are no great hornbills or drongos living wild in Cornwall and, secondly, it is a bit tricky catching birds with a ...

fluffy tail!

"Well, maybe climbing animals are easier to catch than birds?" thinks Bagheera. "I could hunt for a loris or perhaps a macaque".

There are, of course, two main problems here.

Firstly, there are no lorises or macaques living in the wilds of Cornwall.

Secondly, it is rather tricky hunting up trees with a ...

HUGE

"Oh dear, perhaps something nearer the ground will be easier - a python or maybe a king cobra", wonders Bagheera.

There's obviously the two main problems.

Firstly, the lack of pythons and king cobras living wild in Cornwall and, secondly, catching them is somewhat tricky with a ...

Fluffy tail!

"A smaller creature is the answer - how about a tarantula or a scorpion?" thinks Bagheera.

What do you think are the biggest problems now?

You're right!

Firstly, there are (hopefully) no tarantulas or scorpions living wild in Cornwall and, secondly, of course even little things are not easy to deal with when you have a ...

...HUGE

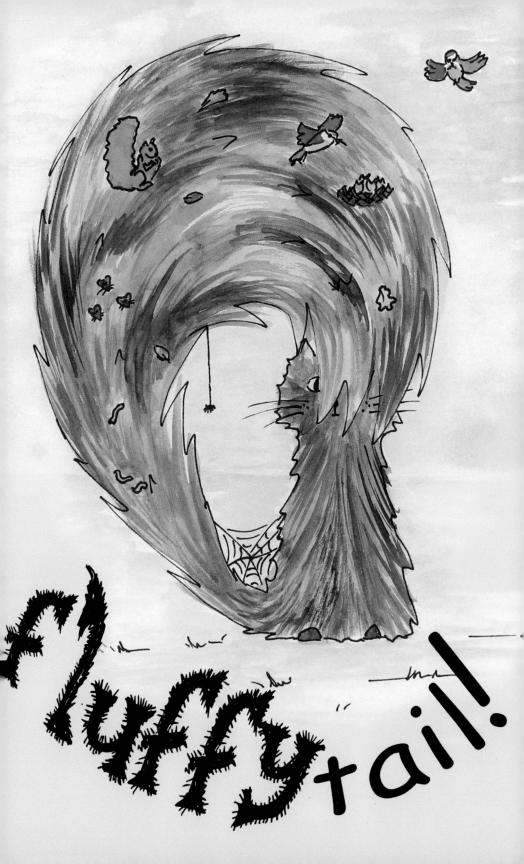

It is rather late now and Bagheera is getting very tired after all his hunting.

"Time to go home for a nap in front of the fire. Maybe I"ll be luckier tomorrow" he thinks.

Poor Bagheera! What a shame he didn't catch anything today!

Our Bagheera stories are inspired by the adventures of our pet cat Bagheera. He frequently comes home carrying twigs, leaves, slugs and all kinds of interesting things in his big fluffy tail.

Bagheera was named after the fictional character in Rudyard Kipling's Jungle Book stories. The Hindi word Bagheera means tiger-like but our Bagheera isn't a bit like a tiger!

Printed in Great Britain
by Amazon